DEAR MOOSE FRIENDS, WELCOME TO THE

STONE AGE!

WELCOME TO THE STONE AGE . . . AND THE WORLD OF THE CAVEMICE!

CAPITAL: OLD MOUSE CITY

POPULATION: WE'RE NOT SURE. (MATH DOESN'T EXIST YET!) BUT BESIDES CAVEMICE, THERE ARE PLENTY OF DINOSAURS, <u>WAY</u> TOO MANY SABER-TOOTHED TIGERS, AND FEROCIOUS CAVE BEARS — BUT NO MOUSE HAS EVER HAD THE COURAGE TO COUNT THEM!

TYPICAL FOOD: PETRIFIED CHEESE SOUP

NATIONAL HOLIDAY: **GREAT ZAP DAY**, WHICH CELEBRATES THE DISCOVERY OF FIRE. RODENTS EXCHANGE GRILLED CHEESE SANDWICHES ON THIS HOLIDAY.

NATIONAL DRINK: MAMMOTH MILKSHAKES

CLIMATE: Unpredictable, WITH FREQUENT METEOR SHOWERS

cheese soup

milkshake

MONEY

SEASHELLS OF ALL SHAPES AND SIZES

MEASUREMENT

THE BASIC UNIT OF MEASUREMENT IS BASED ON THE LENGTH OF THE TAIL OF THE LEADER OF THE VILLAGE. A UNIT CAN BE DIVIDED INTO A HALF TAIL OR QUARTER TAIL. THE LEADER IS ALWAYS READY TO PRESENT HIS TAIL WHEN THERE IS A DISPUTE.

THE CAVEMICE

Geronimo

Trap

Thea

Benjamin

Bugsy Wugsy

Hercule Poirat

Grandma Ratrock

Geronimo Stilton

CAVEMICE

WATCH YOUR TAIL!

Scholastic Inc.

ISBN 978-0-545-44775-1

Based on an original idea by Elisabetta Dami.

www.geronimostilton.com

Published by Scholastic Inc., 557 Broadway, New York, NY 10012. SCHOLASTIC and associated logos are trademarks and/or registered trademarks of Scholastic Inc.

Text by Geronimo Stilton
Original title *Attenti alla coda, meteoriti in arrivo*
Cover by Flavio Ferron
Illustrations by Giuseppe Facciotto (design) and Daniele Verzini (color)
Graphics by Marta Lorini

Special thanks to Tracey West
Translated by Emily Clement
Interior design by Becky James

12 11 10 9 8 7 6 5 4 3 2 1   13 14 15 16 17 18/0

Printed in the U.S.A.   40
First printing, May 2013

MANY AGES AGO, ON PREHISTORIC MOUSE ISLAND, THERE WAS A VILLAGE CALLED OLD MOUSE CITY. IT WAS INHABITED BY BRAVE *RODENT SAPIENS* KNOWN AS THE CAVEMICE.

DANGERS SURROUNDED THE MICE AT EVERY TURN: EARTHQUAKES, METEOR SHOWERS, FEROCIOUS DINOSAURS, AND FIERCE GANGS OF SABER-TOOTHED TIGERS. BUT THE BRAVE CAVEMICE FACED IT ALL WITH A SENSE OF HUMOR, AND WERE ALWAYS READY TO LEND A HAND TO OTHERS.

HOW DO I KNOW THIS? I DISCOVERED AN ANCIENT BOOK WRITTEN BY MY ANCESTOR, GERONIMO STILTONOOT! HE CARVED HIS STORIES INTO STONE TABLETS AND ILLUSTRATED THEM WITH HIS ETCHINGS.

I AM PROUD TO SHARE THESE STONE AGE STORIES WITH YOU. THE EXCITING ADVENTURES OF THE CAVEMICE WILL MAKE YOUR FUR STAND ON END, AND THE JOKES WILL TICKLE YOUR WHISKERS! HAPPY READING!

Geronimo Stilton

WARNING! DON'T IMITATE THE CAVEMICE. WE'RE NOT IN THE STONE AGE ANYMORE!

METEOR SHOWER IN OLD MOUSE CITY!

Dawn fell over *Old Mouse City*, the great village of the **CAVEMICE**. (Well, we think it's great, anyway!)

The first rays of sunlight, as **yellow** as cheese, shone across the entrance to my cave. I had a full day of **HARD** work ahead of me — work as **HARD** as the stone I have to carve all day to write news articles.

But I, **GERONIMO STILTONOOT**, was still asleep in my cozy straw bed. I rolled on my side and continued to snore loudly.

Zzzzzz snooore zzzzz

I was dreaming that I had won a battle against the FEROCIOUS saber-toothed tigers. Everyone was calling me a **hero** and showering me with grated cheese. Suddenly, a shriek as sharp as the claw of a T. rex shattered my eardrums:

"METEOR SHOWER COMING TO OLD MOUSE CITY!"

I recognized that shriek immediately: It was the weathersaurus, a dinosaur that predicts the weather.

A moment later, a tremendous thump shook the walls of my cave. **Bam! Bam! Bam!** This wasn't just a meteor shower — it was a meteor storm!

"Great rocky boulders!" I cried, **jumping** up. "This flying reptile makes useless predictions. He doesn't announce something until it's already happening!"

I leaned out of the entrance of my cave and saw the **meteors** falling like giant hailstones.

"Anyone could make predictions like that," I grumbled.

Bam! Another meteor fell right in front of me, missing me by a whisker!

I tumbled *BACKWARD*, and the weathersaurus

laughed at me.

"Close one!" he said. "And now that you're done **complaining**, I'll tell you my next prediction. There's going to be an earthq —"

Before he could even finish the word, the ground started to **SHAKE** under my feet!

It missed me by a whisker!

THE GREAT ZAP!

I ran back into my cave to save my precious knickknacks. With my left **paw**, I grabbed the **RARE** clay vase that my grandma Ratrock had given me. With my right paw, I grabbed the portrait of *Clarissa Conjurat*, the most fascinating mouse in the village. (I must admit, I am **head over tail** for her. But she doesn't know it — I'm very **shy**!)

My paws were full, but I still had more to grab!

With one foot, I grabbed my secret stash of **seashells** (cavemouse money), and with the other foot, my pet fish **ROCKY'S** bowl.

I was practically juggling!

From outside the cave, the weathersaurus squealed again. "Almost forgot. I'm also predicting a **volcanic eruption**!"

ARGH! A volcanic eruption was the last thing I needed.

I went outside and saw a river of Sizzling lava flowing like hot cheese sauce down the street.

I had to watch my tail or it would get singed!

Then the weathersaurus had one last prediction: "Beware the Great —"

OH, NO! He couldn't mean . . .

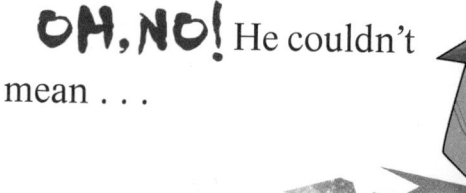

Just as I had feared, the Great Zap struck me.

Then the weathersaurus cheerfully flew away.

"Happy to be of help!" he called.

I shook my head at his nerve. Then I went back into my cave, whiskers SCORCHED and SMOKE coming out of my ears. To console myself, I went into the kitchen and prepared a lovely cheese omelette with a side of meat for **breakfast**. All that stress had made me hungry!

THE GREAT ZAP

The Great Zap is what the cavemice call a powerful flash of lightning. It was named when it once struck a tree and set it ablaze, which led the cavemice to discover fire.

AARGH! The Great Zap!

OW! OW! IT HURTS!

I sat down at the table and bit into my delicious cheese omelette, which I had made with some tasty **swamp** herbs. I reached for a glass of water, but then I remembered that the pipe connecting my cave to the nearest well was **broken**. So I settled for a horsetail* smoothie and a **calming** cup of fern* juice.

I felt like I needed a bath, but of course I couldn't take one without WATER. Also, it wasn't flea-picking day, the one day of the month when cavemice get clean.

* Horsetail and ferns are plants that existed in the prehistoric era and survive to the present day.

I brushed off my forest-green shirt and saw a big group of **prehistoric fleas** jumping all over it. It was Zif and Zaf and their 357 children.

I *politely* said hello to them, and they joyfully returned my greeting. (I've given up trying to chase them away — they always come back!)

Before leaving, I checked my *will*, just in case I became extinct that day.

Life in the Stone Age is very, very hard. As hard as **GRANITE**!

The meteor shower was still going on, so I grabbed my **METEOR UMBRELLA**. It is made of strong stone, and I staggered under its weight.

The meteor umbrella was the most recent creation of **LEO EDISTONE**, the village's inventor. He told me it would keep meteors off me perfectly.

I slowly walked through the streets of Old Mouse City while meteors of all sizes fell around me. Some were as tiny as a crumb of cheese, and some were as huge as a **megalosaurus** egg!

I noticed that all the other mice were

swiftly running down the village streets, and not just because of the **meteors**.

Everyone in Old Mouse City, in fact, was running to their caves, grabbing their stomachs, and moaning.

"Ow! Ow!"

"What a stomachache!"

"HAS THE GREAT PLAGUE RETURNED?"

What is going on? I wondered.

I wasn't able to ask anyone, though, because in the next moment, an enormouse meteor fell right on my meteor umbrella! The umbrella smacked into my head and **DROVE** me into the ground like a hammer driving a nail.

I was stuck! This **METEOR UMBRELLA** was no good at all!

Great rocky boulders, I was such a fool!

Leo Edistone had tricked me into buying one of his useless inventions! And to think I paid thirty **seashells** for it!

I wasn't going to let that crackpot inventor take advantage of me. I wanted my money back!

EDISTONE'S UNUSUAL INVENTIONS

As soon as I climbed out of the **hole** in the ground, I **hurried** to Leo Edistone's workshop with my meteor umbrella in my paw. On the street, I was stopped by a rodent who was distributing **FLYERS** for the new clinic run by the **Club brothers**. I took a look at the flyer. What great timing they had! The brothers must have already made a fortune off the **stomachache** epidemic.

Take this!

The Club Brothers' Clinic
Let Us Help You!

HAVE A STOMACHACHE? TOOTHACHE? PAW PROBLEMS?

At our clinic, we can take care of anything — even a dinosaur bite! How do we do it? With the Club Brothers' Cure-All! A secret treatment passed down by our dear old grandmother. With new methods of local and general anesthesia, you won't feel a thing!

LOCAL ANESTHESIA: SMALL BOP ON THE HEAD

GENERAL ANESTHESIA: LARGE BOP ON THE HEAD

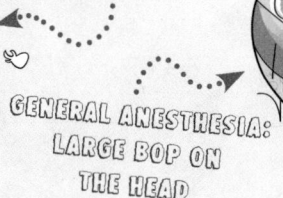

SPECIAL OFFER:
Today only we are offering a discount on the cure for terrible stomachaches! Each Cure-All treatment is only twenty shells!

TELL YOUR FRIENDS THAT THE CLUB BROTHERS CURED YOU!

My thoughts were interrupted by a loud **CLANG! CLANG! CLANG!** coming from Leo's workshop.

As I walked across the flimsy BRIDGE to his rickety home, the logs the bridge was made of started to **move**. I flailed my arms, trying to keep my balance, but I slipped! I fell into the WATER with a loud splash.

This bridge doesn't look too safe to me. . . .

LEO EDISTONE
VILLAGE INVENTOR

HE IS THE BRILLIANT AND MISUNDERSTOOD INVENTOR OF OLD MOUSE CITY.

HIS DREAM IS FOR HIS INVENTIONS TO MAKE LIFE EASIER FOR THE CAVEMICE.

HIS SECRET: HE ALWAYS SMELLS A LITTLE LIKE WILD ONIONS . . . BUT DON'T EVEN THINK ABOUT MENTIONING IT TO HIM!

WILD ONION

Leo appeared at the entrance to his workshop. "Hey, Geronimo!" he called out. "Why are you swimming in my **SWAMP**?"

I shot him an angry look as I picked swampweed from my wet fur.

"I'll fish you out right away!" he yelled. He used a hook attached to the end of a branch to pluck me out of the **muddy** water and pull me into his dry workshop.

Leo is a thin mouse with a long, gray beard, and is always full of energy. His eyes **sparkled** as he asked me, "So, what do you think of my moving walkway?"

"MOVING WALKWAY?" I repeated, dumbfounded. "What is it, a device to get rid of unsatisfied customers?"

Leo shrugged. "Well, a moving walkway could transport people in an **AIRPORT**, when they have heavy **LUGGAGE**."

"Airport? Luggage? What are those?" I asked.

"New ideas!" he replied, his eyes twinkling again. "If those things already existed, my moving walkway would be very useful. Believe me, one day this will be useful to all kinds of mice, especially elderly rodents."

My anger toward the inventor faded away. At heart, all he really wanted to do was improve the lives of others. So I decided not to ask for my **seashells** back.

Instead, I said, "I've come to return your meteor umbrella."

"Why?" Leo asked, surprised.

"It doesn't work!" I informed him. "When a

meteor hit me, it **POUNDED** me into the ground. Maybe it's good for keeping off the **rain**, but that's about it."

Leo lit up. "Why, that's a great idea!" he said. "If I can make it LIGHTER, it would be perfect for shielding rodents from the rain. Geronimo, I ought to make you my **assistant**!"

"Um, no, thank you," I said quickly. "I'm very **busy** with my job at *The Stone Gazette*."

The inventor nodded. "Well, then, in exchange for the meteor umbrella, you can take any other invention you like!" he **exclaimed**. "Go on!"

Then he led me to his **closet of inventions**....

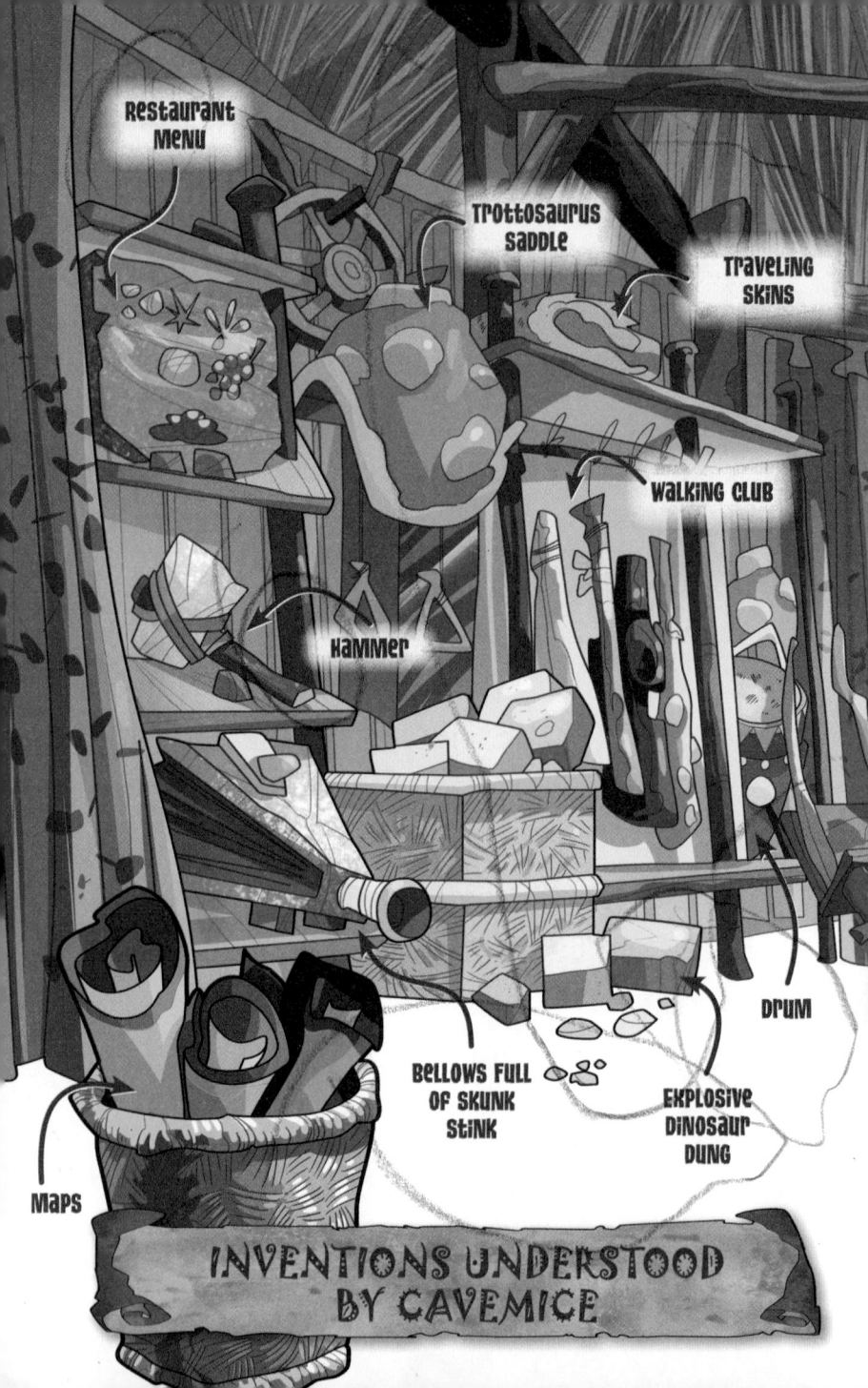

RESTAURANT MENU

TROTTOSAURUS SADDLE

TRAVELING SKINS

WALKING CLUB

HAMMER

DRUM

MAPS

BELLOWS FULL OF SKUNK STINK

EXPLOSIVE DINOSAUR DUNG

INVENTIONS UNDERSTOOD BY CAVEMICE

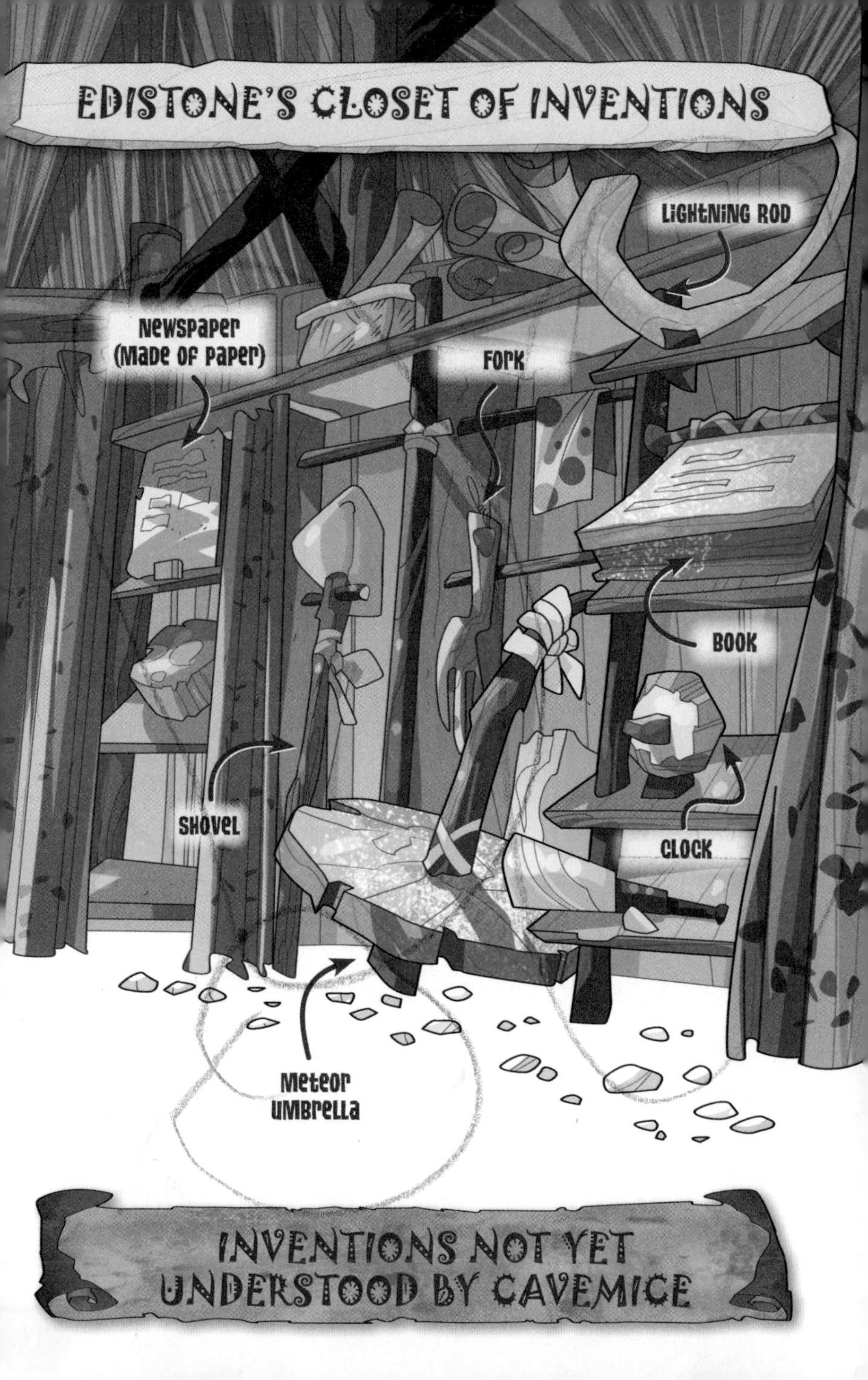

EDISTONE'S CLOSET OF INVENTIONS

LIGHTNING ROD

NEWSPAPER
(MADE OF PAPER)

FORK

BOOK

SHOVEL

CLOCK

METEOR
UMBRELLA

INVENTIONS NOT YET
UNDERSTOOD BY CAVEMICE

NOW, THAT'S AN IDEA!

Leo proudly showed me his new inventions. I was impressed by the bricks of explosive dinosaur dung, which could be used to start a fire without WOOD.

"I sold this invention to a poor rodent who had never been warm the previous winter," he said with a little sigh. Then his eyes got bright again as he pointed to a new shelf. "These inventions will help us DEFEND against the saber-toothed tigers. The bellows are full of

skunk stink to assault their sensitive noses. The **scratching powder** will make them itch unbearably. And of course, this **Superbean Concentrate** powers our balloonosauruses."

Then he moved to the other side of the closet, and his voice became sad. "This, on the other hand, is my closet of **Not-Yet-Understood Inventions**. I cannot release them yet because the world is not ready to **accept** them!"

He got a dreamy look in his eyes. "I just hope that the day will come when all rodents will realize how useful these objects are."

Then he handed me a strange **STONE** object.

"What do you think of this, eh?" he asked.

The object was a tall, narrow piece of stone stuck in the center of a round, flat **STONE**.

"Um, it's amazing," I said. **But what is it?**

"It's a sundial, of course!" he cheerfully replied. "It tells time!"

"**Tells time?**" I repeated, confused.

He shook his head sadly.

It tells time!

What's time?

"Such a shame!" he sighed. "I was hoping that you, an **intellectual** mouse, would understand this invention!"

He frowned, thinking. "Hmm . . . hmm . . . **I think I've got it!** I have another invention to show you."

He rummaged through the shelves, MUTTERING, "Where could I have put it?"

"Um, what are you looking for?" I asked.

"You'll see," he promised. "**Aha!** This is the perfection invention for you."

He held out a block of thin, rectangular stones held together with strips of leather.

"It's a stone **book**!" he exclaimed.

He passed me the book, but I fumbled it, and it dropped right on my foot!

"**AAAAH!**" I squealed. "That hurt!"

He looked disappointed. "You don't want my book? Such a shame! Just think: You could carve something into it. You know, like recipes . . . or stories!"

"Stories?" I repeated, curious. "Like the

Take it! It's a gift!

Aaaah!

ones our **elders** have told around the **fire**? What a wonderful idea!"

I took the heavy book, thanked Leo, and headed for *The Stone Gazette*. In the streets, a chorus of advertising **squealers** squawked loudly:

"Don't worry about your stomachache! Call the Club brothers and you'll be back in good shape!"

SOUND THE TOM-TOM ALARM!

When I finally arrived at the offices of *The Stone Gazette,* not a single mouse was **CHISELING** away on the next issue. They were all home with a stomachache! Only my sister, Thea, was there, but she was about to go home **sick**, too.

As she was leaving, she noticed the object I was carrying. "What's that?" she asked.

"It's one of Edistone's new inventions!" I responded proudly. "It's called a '**book**.' You can carve stories in it!"

"Stories? Like the ones our elders tell us?" Thea asked. "Why would we need to **CARVE** them down?"

"So that we don't forget the stories that make us **laugh** and dream," I replied. "Like that story Grandma Ratrock always tells about getting stuck in the pit of **melted** cheese. If we carve it into a book, we can read it again and again."

"That's an interesting idea," she said, but then she turned pale.
"I feel sick, Geronimo.
Gotta go!"

I'll carve stories into it!

37

I went into my **OFFICE** and decided to test out Edistone's new invention by carving an article into it. Suddenly, the sound of the emergency tom-tom rang through the village!

TOM-TO-TOM! TOM-TO-TOM! TOM-TO-TOM!
TOM-TO-TOM! TOM-TO-TOM! TOM-TO-TOM!

It was an urgent message from our village leader, ErneST HeFtymouSe.

Here is the message:

"EMERGENCY! MEET IMMEDIATELY IN SINGING STONE SQUARE! IF ANYONE ARRIVES LATE, I WILL TIE YOUR TAIL IN A KNOT!"

I hurried out of *The Stone Gazette* offices and ran toward the square. I like my tail just the way it is, thank you!

CONSIDER YOURSELF EXTINCT, GERONIMO!

In the square, everyone was moaning about how bad they felt.

"Ow, ow, ow!"

"My tummy hurts!"

"I haven't been able to eat anything all day!"

"ME, NEITHER!"

The village leader, Ernest Heftymouse, addressed the crowd.

"Citizens!" he declared. "We have an **EMERGENCY**! Every last mouse in the village has a stomachache!"

I raised my paw. "Actually, I'm just **fine**."

Everyone gathered around me, shocked.

"YOU'RE NOT SICK? REALLY?"

The chief and his wife, Chattina, came up to me. Ernest poked me in the **stomach**. "Hmm, strange," he muttered. "Why aren't you sick?"

I shrugged apologetically. "Um . . . I have no idea!"

Why don't you have a stomachache?

Ernest turned to the crowd.

"Residents of Old Mouse City!" he began again. "An unknown **danger** is threatening us. This stomachache could make us all **extinct**! But don't worry, I have an idea!"

"Hooray!" exclaimed the villagers.

Ernest raised a paw in the air. "We will call on our shaman, Bluster Conjurat!"

"Waaaaaah!" the cavemice wailed in disappointment. Our shaman is often not very helpful.

Bluster Conjurat **SLOWLY** made his way through the crowd. The elderly rodent had gray fur, a **wrinkled** face, and a very long **WHITE** beard. In his right paw, he held a **STICK** with three colorful shells attached to the top.

Everyone moved out of his way and exchanged **nervous** looks.

44

"Shaman Bluster Conjurat!" Ernest addressed him. "In your great wisdom, what do you suggest that we do?"

The shaman waved his arms and spoke in a mysterious voice. "I, SHAMAN BLUSTER CONJURAT, I see . . . I see . . . that if we don't do something soon, we'll all go **extinct**!"

This situation is serious!

Chattina Heftymouse impatiently stomped her foot. "We already knew that!"

A murmur went through the crowd.

"**SILENCE!**" Bluster shouted. "Or **THE GREAT ZAP** will strike you all! I see . . . I see . . . a mouse that doesn't have a **stomachache** . . ."

Chattina snorted. "We already knew that, too! It's **GERONIMO STILTONOOT**!"

The shaman shuffled up to me, squinted, and then pointed. "Yes! He is that mouse. He is the chosen one who will save us!"

"**Chosen one?**" I repeated with disbelief. That didn't sound good. "Um . . . what do you mean, 'chosen one'?"

Conjurat stomped his walking stick on the ground and made his next pronouncement very **loudly**.

"Since you are the only one who is not sick,

you are the only one who can complete a **DANGEROUS MISSION**. You must find . . ."

Everyone held their breath.

"The recipe for the potion that will cure the **Great Stomachache**!"

You are the chosen one!

M-me?

The crowd gasped.

"Now come to my cave so I can prepare you for your **MISSION**," Bluster told me.

I tried to slip away, but Chattina grabbed me by the **ear** to drag me back to Bluster. "Where do you think you're going?" she asked.

My friends all felt sorry for me. They knew I was heading into **DANGER**.

"Poor Geronimo . . ."

"We love you so much!"

"You've always been so good to us!"

Even my friend Hercule Poirat, the famouse detective, was sobbing on my behalf.

The worry of my friends made me even more afraid. I headed to Bluster's cave with trembling paws.

We'll miss you so much!

THE SHAMAN'S CAVE

I was so anxious about going that Chattina had to push me into Bluster's **CAVE**. Inside, the air was **damp** and heavy, with the strong smell of **medicinal** herbs.

As soon as my eyes got used to the darkness, I noticed a **fire pit** in the center of the cave. Baskets full of **berries**, seeds, and dried flowers hung from the ceilings. Strange **CEREMONIAL** masks decorated the walls.

Suddenly, a lighted **T⚡RCH** appeared right in front of me, and I felt a paw brush against my face.

"There you are, finally," someone said in a whisper.

"Ahhh!" I screamed. "Wh-who are you? A *ghost*?"

"Don't be such a scaredy-mouse," the voice scolded me.

The torch moved aside, and I saw before me the most beautiful face in the entire village. It belonged to *Clarissa*, the intelligent and charming daughter of the shaman.

Clarissa looked at me with eyes as GRAY as stone and deep as the ST⚡RMY sky.

"Geronimo, are you happy I'm here, too?"

My legs felt as *wobbly* as a bowl of cheese custard. I could barely speak!

Clarissa Conjurat

EYES: GRAY AS STONE

HAIR: PINK AND FLOWING

PERSONALITY: DETERMINED AND FIRM, BUT AS SWEET AS CHEESECAKE. SHE ALWAYS GETS WHAT SHE WANTS.

HOBBY: IN HER FREE TIME, SHE TAMES WILD DINOSAURS.

PET PEEVE: SHE HATES BAD SMELLS, SO SHE SPRAYS EVERYTHING WITH LILY WATER!

I was so nervous I started breaking out in **ᴚed** and **white** spots, as if I were a dinosaur with **measles**.

"Y-yes, I'm h-happy you're here, Clarissa," I stammered.

I tried to politely **kiss** her paw, but she gave me a very firm handshake instead. **WHAT A RODENT!**

Then the shaman walked into the cave.

"**Ahem!**" Bluster said with a cough. "My dear victim . . . I mean, **CHOSEN ONE**. Let us begin!

"As a shaman, I can **see** things no cavemouse could ever imagine,"

Ah!

Are you happy I'm here?

Bluster continued. Then he winked at me. "For example, I can see from the look on your face that you admire my daughter, Clarissa."

I **blushed**, and he laughed. "Ha, ha! But I don't need special powers to see that you two are not right for each other. She's as tough as GRANITE, while you are as soft as melted cheese."

Um ... that's true!

My whiskers drooped: He was right. I would never win over Clarissa!

"However, there may be one way to impress my daughter," Bluster said, *LEANING* close to whisper to me. "If you can complete your **MISSION** — without going extinct, of course — she just might notice you!"

Then he looked at his daughter. "Clarissa,

55

what do you think of our **CHOSEN ONE**?" he asked. "Will he return alive?"

She looked me over from the tips of my whiskers to the end of my tail. Then she gave my arm a squeeze.

"Well, he doesn't have much in the way of **MUSCLES**," she declared. "But he's very smart, and that might help him succeed."

She picked up a bowl of **Strange green liquid**, dipped a finger into it, and spread the muck on my face.

"There! A little bit of **sweet** lily water for you. I love **LiLies**!" she said. Then she sniffed the air and frowned. "I think your **moldy prehistoric** fur needs a double dose."

And with that, she dumped the entire contents of the bowl on my head.

I was speechless. I was covered from head to tail with the sticky **green goop**!

But the last thing I wanted to do was argue with Clarissa, so I simply gave her a big, goofy **smile**.

Bluster approached and waved his arms. "It is time, Chosen One, to go to the Cave of Memories. There you will find the secret recipe for the potion that will cure the Great Stomachache. The

That's better!

recipe is hidden in the most mysterious and dangerous part of the cave."

"Dad, no rodent has ever returned alive from the cave!" Clarissa **protested**. "And this chosen one doesn't even have any **MUSCLES**!"

"Don't worry," the shaman replied, "I'll strengthen him with one of my potions. Let's see, I'll need some codfish scales and some STINGING NETTLE powder, but what's that last ingredient?"

He fumbled through the jars on his shelves. "Maybe it was cave-bear fur, or tears of a toad, or **BAT BONES**," he muttered. Finally, he threw up his paws. "Oh, well, we'll just let the victim . . . I mean, the chosen one . . . taste it, and we'll see what effect it has!"

I watched Buster throw handfuls of smelly herbs and powders into a bowl. I had no intention of drinking any potion of his, but he pinched my snout and forced a spoonful of the **disgusting** stuff down my throat.

"Drink up!" he ordered.

I LIKE ... YOU!

I started to feel **itchy** right away. Then my whole body started blowing up like a **BALLOON**!

Bluster shook his head. "*How strange!*" he muttered. "Victim . . . I mean, Chosen One . . . I will make you a new **potion**!"

With that, he gave me one **NEW** potion after another, watching each time to see what would happen.

"Well, do you feel **STRONGER**?" he asked. "No? Oh, well. I wonder what's missing from this disgusting brew . . . I mean, this *miraculous potion* . . . Let me try a new mix."

He was never going to get it right!

Finally, before he could make me gulp down something else, I pushed away and yelled, **"NO MORE POTIONS!"**

I felt better. Much, much better. And as **STRONG** as a cave bear!

Clarissa gave me a pat on the back so hard it would have knocked over a **T. REX**.

"Well done, Chosen One!" she exclaimed. "I like these traits on you. You're **BRAVE** . . . adventurous . . . and smelling like a flower!"

I couldn't believe my ears. Had she really said, "**I like . . . you**"? Okay, so maybe she didn't exactly say, "Geronimo, I like you," but it was pretty close.

Bluster Conjurat had known exactly how to get me to accept his mission. Just the thought that Clarissa might like me was enough to send me heading into terrible **DANGER**!

"C-Clarissa," I stammered. "Maybe when

we come back from this mission, you could join me for some **cheese** fondue."

"I prefer a nice hunk of **roasted meat**," she replied. "But anyway, I'm not sure that you *will* come back from this mission!"

My heart **sank**. "I shouldn't have asked."

Then she winked at me. "If you do survive the cave, I'll think about it," she said. "I do like reading your newspaper."

She liked reading my newspaper! What a compliment! My **heart** was flying higher than a **balloonosaurus**.

Bluster shoved a map into my hands.

"Go, oh Chosen One! And return with the recipe!"

I took the **MAP**, and Clarissa and I left the cave. We were saying good-bye when a giant paw **GRABBED** me by the tail. It was the paw of Harriet Heftymouse, the daughter of the village chief.

"My dear **Geronimo-mo**!" she chirped. "You are so brave to leave on such a dangerous mission. Remember that a delicate and defenseless mouse will be awaiting your return."

Geronimo-mo!

Harriet Heftymouse

"Who are you talking about?" I asked, perplexed.

"Me, of course!" she squeaked.

64

I thought that maybe the **Great Stomachache** was affecting Harriet's mind. Delicate and defenseless? She is much **STRONGER** than I am!

Clarissa looked curious. "Are you two dating?" she asked.

I **blushed**. I barely knew Harriet, and I didn't go out on a lot of dates. I am always too busy working at *The Stone Gazette*.

"No, no!" I answered.

Then Ernest Heftymouse arrived and **squeezed** me in a suffocating hug.

"What a fine son-in-law you'll make, Chosen One!" he said.

Welcome to the family!

Son-in-law? Harriet and I weren't even dating. Who said anything about **marriage**?

"You can live in our **CAVE**," Ernest went on. "It's the finest in the village! And I'll give you a new **club**, too. What do you say?"

I was about to protest when Chattina ran up.

"You'll be such a *wonderful* part of the family," she gushed. "And I've already thought of your wedding present. A **cheese sculpture** of you and your lovely bride! Won't that be marvelous?"

"Everybody stop!" I yelled. "There's not going to be a wedding! I do not want to marry Harriet!"

Unfortunately, no one heard me, because everyone's stomachache had suddenly returned. They all *ran off* quickly.

I was finally alone!

Then a paw whacked me on the back, and I heard a familiar voice. "Cousin!"

I turned, surprised. "**Trap?** I thought you were on vacation!"

A VERY DANGEROUS MISSION!

My cousin Trap took me by the arm. "I was on **vacation**, but I just returned," he explained happily. "And just in time to learn about your **MISSION**. The whole **VILLAGE** is talking about it!"

I'll come with you!

I sighed. "Yeah, I'm **STUCK** doing it. And now I really need to get going, and . . ."

Trap didn't let me finish.

"This Great Stomachache is bad for business at my ROTTEN TOOTH TAVERN," Trap went on, "so I decided I might as well go with you. Speaking of which, WHERE exactly are we going?"

I looked at the sky and sighed, **defeated**. Whenever Trap gets involved, things usually become a **mess**. But I reluctantly agreed to him coming. I know that when Trap gets an idea into his head, it's impossible to make him change his mind!

"I need to go to this MYSTERIOUS cave," I explained. "See, the route is marked here."

I unrolled the **MAP** that Buster had drawn on a banana leaf for me. When I started to read the terrifying names of the places I would need to cross, I turned as pale as mozzarella!

1. **OLD MOUSE CITY: start!**
2. **PREHISTORIC VOLCANO: danger of roasting!**
3. **WILD DINOSAUR PLAIN: danger of sharp claws!**
4. **MOSQUITO SWAMP: danger of swarm attack!**
5. **DESERT OF GIANT SCORPIONS: danger of stinging!**

6. WERE-BAT LAIR: **danger of fangs!**
7. SHIFTING SANDS: **danger of sinking!**
8. TIGER CAMP: **danger of being eaten!**
9. FOGGY PASS: **danger of getting lost!**
10. CAVE OF MEMORIES: **danger unknown!**

Shifting sands? Giant scorpions? Were-bats? Wild dinosaurs?

So scary!

"GREAT ROCKY BOULDERS, WE COULD GO EXTINCT ON THIS MISSION!" I exclaimed.

Trap shrugged his shoulders. "Eh, they're just rumors," he said. "You'll see, when we return to Old Mouse City with the **cure** for the Great Stomachache, we'll be greeted as **heroes**!"

Before leaving, we stopped at my cave to get some supplies. I grabbed my club for protection and then packed some provisions: hard **cheese**, soft **cheese**, **CHEESE** sticks, **CHEESE** wheels, **cheese** bread, dried berries and **cheese**, and some

meat with **cheese** sauce.

Finally, I packed a hollow **GOURD** filled with fern juice (since my water pipes were still broken). It was going to be a long journey.

I gave one last look at my cozy cave and **sighed**. Then I left to meet my destiny . . . and, perhaps, my extinction!

DOUBLE LOAD, DOUBLE DOSE!

My **AUTºSAURUS** was parked on the street in front of my cave. Trap and I jumped on board, but he immediately tossed us off.

"I won't do it!" the dinosaur protested. "For a double load, I need a double dose of my **Superfruit Smoothie**!"

I knew I had to give in or he wouldn't take us anywhere. Fortunately, I had a good supply of his smoothie stored up.

He **slurped** it down in an instant, and then we climbed into the saddle. He reared up on his hind legs and took off at a **GALLOP**.

We quickly crossed the empty city and passed the anti-tiger **FENCE**. Then we

followed the shaman's map outside the city limits — and into **UNKNOWN TERRITORY**.

Remember all those **DANGERS** I saw on the map? Well, we soon found out that they weren't just rumors. They were all true!

Let's go!

Squeeeeak!

Let's get out of here!

The **volcano's lava** nearly roasted us. Then a herd of very hungry wild **T. REXES** chased us, trying to chomp our tails. "Quick! Throw them some food!" I yelled.

It was a good plan. The dinos began to **fight** among themselves as they all tried to **devour** it.

Then we got to the swamp, and the meat-eating mosquitoes started to bite our

Don't eat us!

ears. We fought them off with our clubs. Then the **giant scorpions** tried to pinch the legs of my autosaurus, but he ran away.

"Hey, Cousin," Trap said. **"Are we through the danger?"**

I checked the map. "Oh, no! We're entering the lair of the **were-bats**!"

As soon as the words left my mouth,

Gulp!

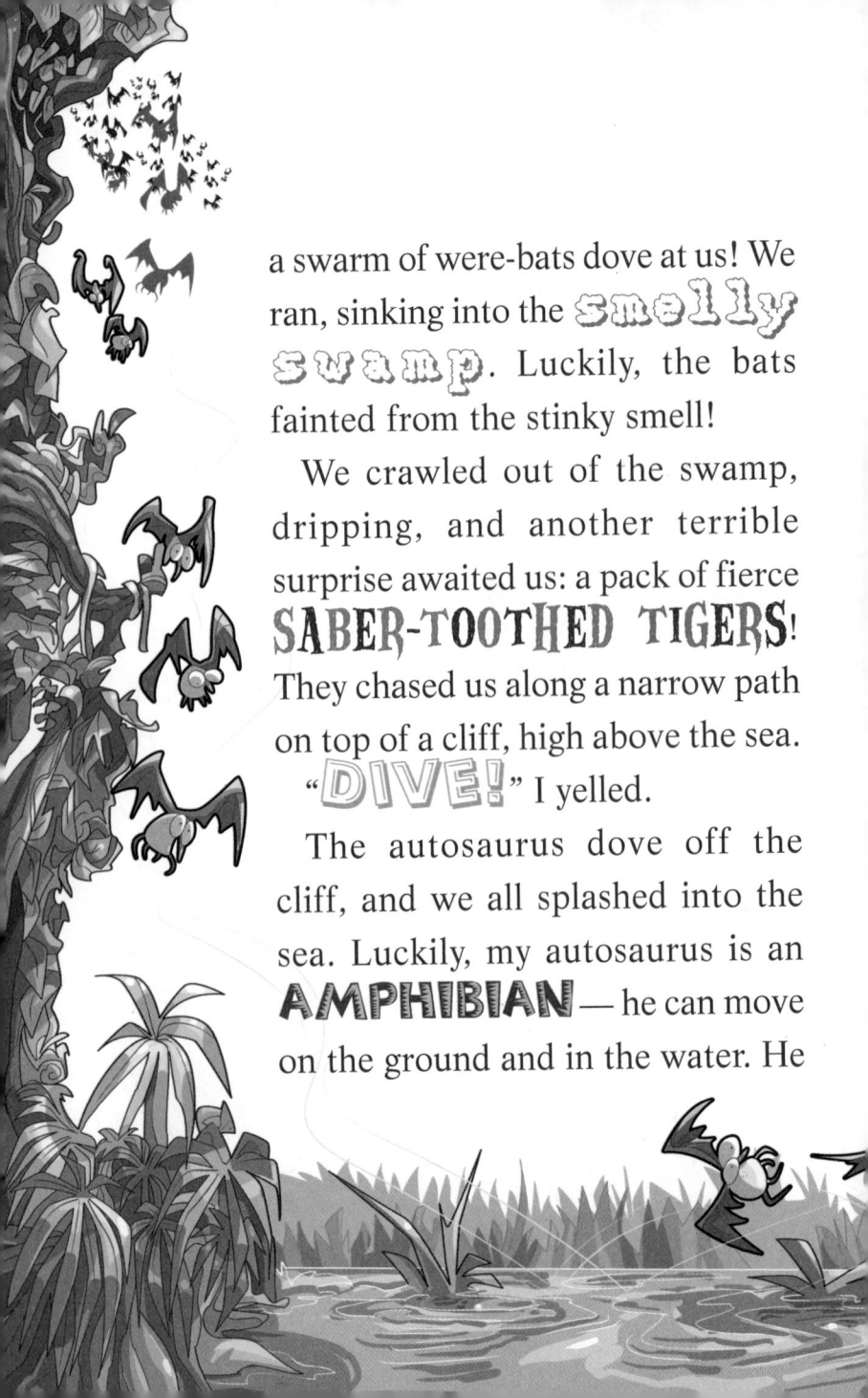

a swarm of were-bats dove at us! We ran, sinking into the **smelly swamp**. Luckily, the bats fainted from the stinky smell!

We crawled out of the swamp, dripping, and another terrible surprise awaited us: a pack of fierce **SABER-TOOTHED TIGERS**! They chased us along a narrow path on top of a cliff, high above the sea.

"**DIVE!**" I yelled.

The autosaurus dove off the cliff, and we all splashed into the sea. Luckily, my autosaurus is an **AMPHIBIAN** — he can move on the ground and in the water. He

paddled through the water, and we landed safely on the beach.

I was lucky that I had chosen a multipurpose model of autosaurus. He had saved us from **early extinction**!

Exhausted from all of the danger, I **fainted**. I soon woke up because my autosaurus was *licking* my face. I hugged him, thinking he was showing me some **affection**, but he shrugged me off.

"I just wanted to be sure you were awake," he said. "I need a triple dose of **Superfruit Smoothie** after all this running and swimming!"

"Welcome back to the living, Cousin," Trap interrupted. "Now, I have good news and

BAD NEWS. Which do you want to hear first?"

"The good news," I replied. "I need to hear something positive!"

Trap grinned. "The good news is that we've finally reached the cave!"

"Then what's the **BAD NEWS**?" I asked.

"The **BAD NEWS** is . . . right in front of us!" Trap said, pointing.

WHAT'S THE PASSWORD?

An enormouse **CAVE BEAR** was sleeping in front of the cave. Trembling, we tiptoed past it, but I stepped on a branch. **SNAP!** The sound woke the bear, who **growled** at us threateningly. His **eyes** were red with fury.

Good Fluffy!

Then we heard a voice. **"DOWN, FLUFFY!"**

The guardian of the cave, a grizzled rodent with a long beard, was perched on a rock.

"Relax, my Fluffy won't

bite," the $guardian$ said. "At least, not unless I ask him to. Ha, ha!"

"Please let us pass," I said, a little nervously. "We are on a mission and need to enter the cave."

The guardian raised an eyebrow. "You may enter — if you know the pAssword."

Password? I started to panic. "Please, just let us enter!" I begged. "Old Mouse City is suffering from the Great Stomachache. I am the chosen one, and I need to find the recipe for the cure."

The **guardian** shook his head. "What's the password? If you don't know it, I will have to set Fluffy on you! He's very **HUNGRY**. He hasn't eaten in days."

Fluffy **drooled**, thinking about his next meal — us!

"**Concentrate**, Cousin!" Trap squealed. "Try to think of the password!"

I closed my eyes and tried to think (which isn't easy to do with a hungry cave bear **drooling** in front of you!).

I tried to remember everything the shaman had said to me. Bluster hadn't mentioned a **pAssword** at all.

"That **SILLY SHAMAN**!" I shrieked. "When I get back — *if* I get back — I'll give him a piece of my mind!"

I had to do something, so I started to shout out random words. "Cave! Swamp! Great rocky boulders! Coconut head!"

The guardian shook his shaggy head once again. "No, that's not it! I guess I'll have to release Fluffy. . . ."

Trap nudged me. "Come on, say it! What are you waiting for? The next ICE AGE?"

But the guardian had already signaled to Fluffy. The cave bear moved toward us, growling. . . .

Terrified, I shouted, "Bluster said nothing about a password. *Nothing!*"

The hermit looked surprised. "What did you say? Did you say 'nothing'? Well done! That's the password!"

Trap and I looked at each other, confused. But at least we were safe.

"DOWN, FLUFFY!" the guardian commanded. "Stay away from the chosen one!"

But the order came too late. **CHOMP!** Fluffy bit the **TIP OF MY TAIL**, itching for a taste of the meal that he was missing.

"Bad Fluffy!" the hermit scolded.

Thankfully, Fluffy then climbed back on top of his rock, pouting.

The guardian gave each of us — including Fluffy — a lit torch.

"Follow me," he said.

We obeyed, keeping a safe distance from Fluffy (we still didn't trust him) as the rodent led us into the Cave of Memories. We walked down a set of stone stairs and found ourselves in an enormouse grotto. Torchlight danced across the walls as we gazed around in awe.

The walls and stone columns were PAINTED with scenes of typical activities of the CAVEMICE: running from dinosaurs, riding on the backs of mammoths, battling tigers . . .

PETRIFIED CHEESE, WHAT AN INCREDIBLE PLACE!

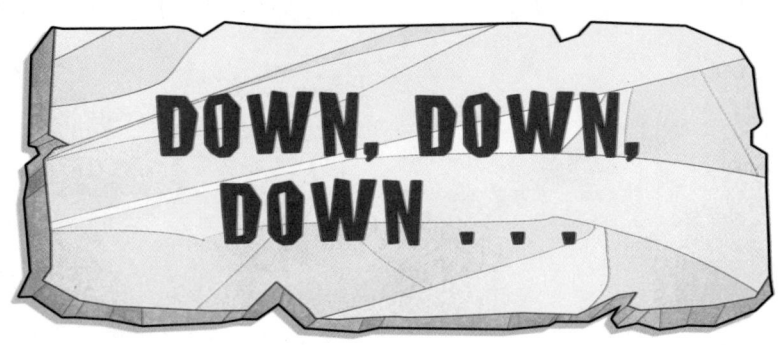

DOWN, DOWN, DOWN . . .

We began to explore the cave, following the **MAP** that Bluster had given me. In the Room of Cave Paintings, all of the most **IMPORTANT MOMENTS** in the history of Old Mouse City had been painted:

THE FIRST STRIKE OF THE GREAT ZAP

THE BIRTH OF THE TWINS WHO FOUNDED THE CITY

THE DISCOVERY OF THE STONE OF FIRE

THE ATTACK OF TIGER KHAN'S HORDE

Then we admired the portraits of the Heftymouse dynasty, which for generations have been leaders of Old Mouse City.

The Heftymouse Dynasty

eat-Great-ndpa Hamlet Heftymouse

Great-Grandpa Hal Heftymouse

Grandpa Hank Heftymouse

Ernest Heftymouse

MAP OF THE CAVE OF MEMORIES

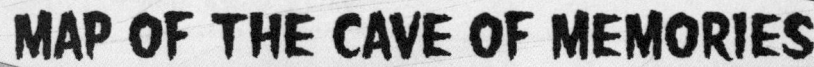

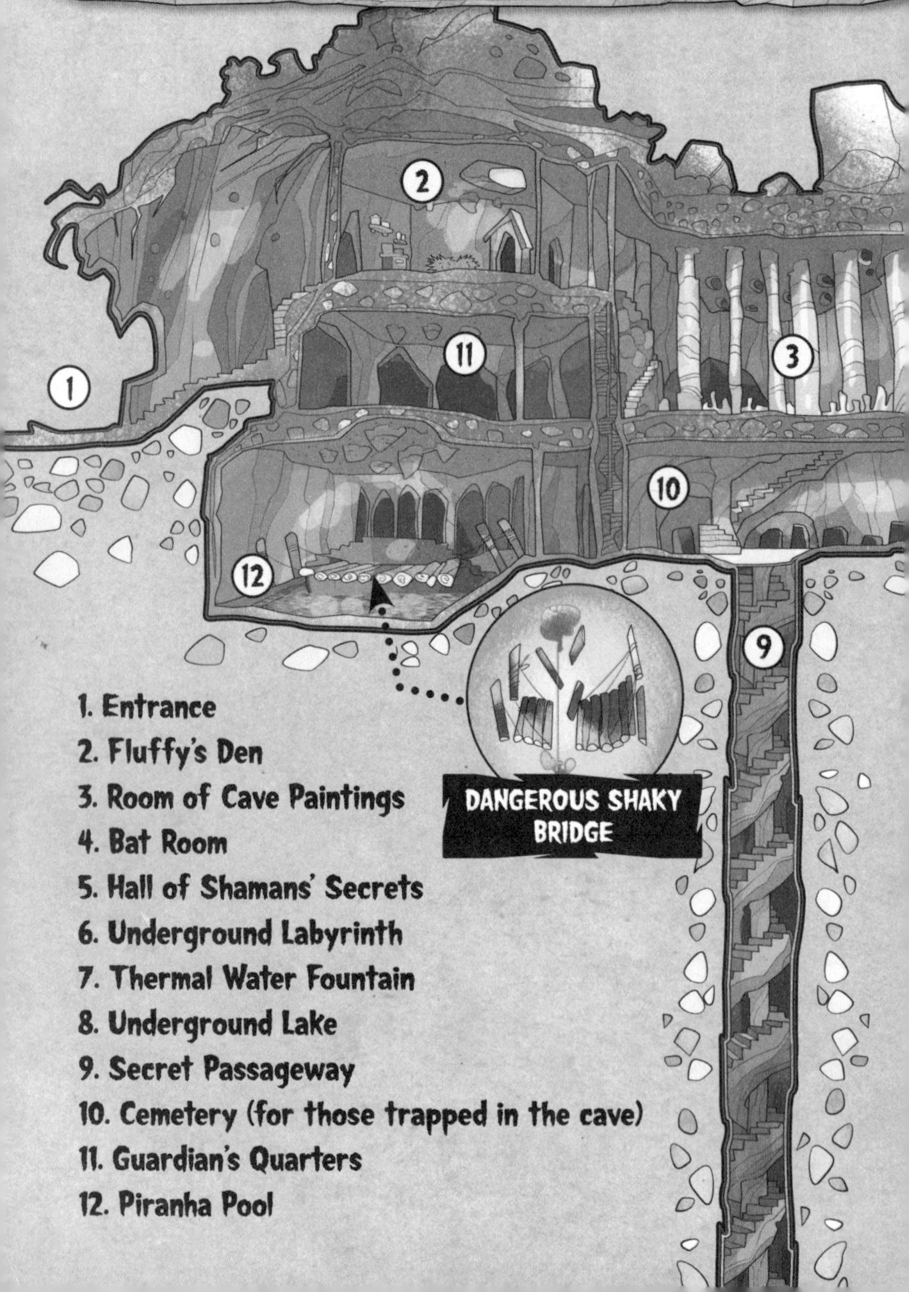
2
11
3
1
10
12
9
DANGEROUS SHAKY BRIDGE

1. Entrance
2. Fluffy's Den
3. Room of Cave Paintings
4. Bat Room
5. Hall of Shamans' Secrets
6. Underground Labyrinth
7. Thermal Water Fountain
8. Underground Lake
9. Secret Passageway
10. Cemetery (for those trapped in the cave)
11. Guardian's Quarters
12. Piranha Pool

DANGEROUS HIDDEN TUNNEL

DANGEROUS FEROCIOUS BATS

DANGEROUS FENCE MADE OF SPEARS

DANGEROUS FALLING BOULDERS

As we left the Room of Cave Paintings, the ground began to shake.

"Quick! *Let's get out of here before everything collapses!*" Trap squealed.

The guardian and Fluffy had already taken off, and we followed them. But a *LANDSLIDE* of rocks crashed down, blocking the exit! We were **TRAPPED**!

Everything's falling!

"**HEEELP!**" I yelled. "We're trapped!"

"Well, at least we're not **alone** in here with Fluffy," Trap said with a laugh.

I found myself laughing, too. "Thanks, Trap. This is what friends are for: making the **best** of a bad situation!"

Just then, I noticed a wind was causing the torch **FLAME** to lean to the right. If there was *wind*, then there had to be another exit!

Our spirits were lifted as we followed the stream of air to a staircase. We walked up the steps and into the **Hall of Shamans' Secrets**!

I shone the torch against the wall, and there it was: the **recipe** we needed for the cure! I began to carefully chisel a copy

into my STONE NOTEBOOK.

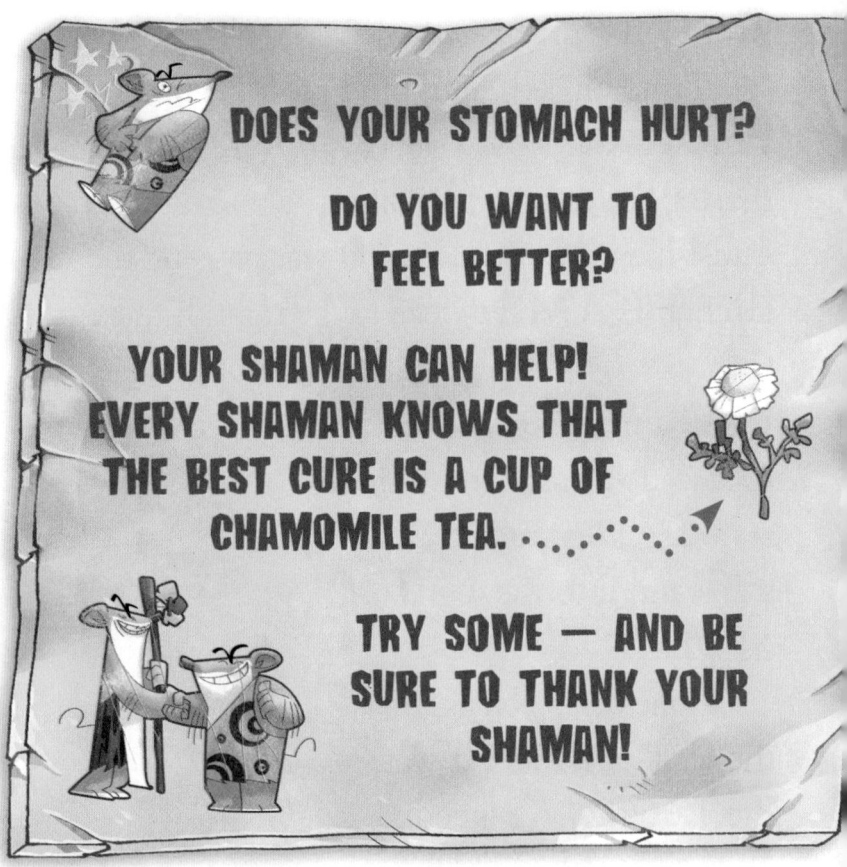

DOES YOUR STOMACH HURT?

DO YOU WANT TO FEEL BETTER?

YOUR SHAMAN CAN HELP! EVERY SHAMAN KNOWS THAT THE BEST CURE IS A CUP OF CHAMOMILE TEA.

TRY SOME — AND BE SURE TO THANK YOUR SHAMAN!

Heeeeeelp!

I finished chiseling and stepped back from the wall. But as soon as my paw touched the ground, I realized that there *was* no ground — I had stepped into a **huge** hole! Trap reached out to grab me, but we both fell **down, down, down.** . . .

Splash!

We landed in **icy** water. We had fallen down a well! My poor whiskers **FROZE** from the cold.

AHHHHHHHHHH!

The stream carried us into a dark **TUNNEL**. Then the stream became a rushing WATERFALL! We plunged **over** the falls and landed in a peaceful underground lake. With the last of our strength, we swam to a small, rocky beach. We flopped onto the shore, finally able to rest.

As we caught our breath, a pale light and the sound of two voices drifted from a tunnel carved into the rock wall next to us.

HºW STRANGe!
Who could it be?

And HºW in the name of cheese did they get here?

We crept into the tunnel and hid behind a boulder to get a better look. I motioned to Trap to stay silent. There, in the light of flickering torches, we could see the faces of the two mysterious mice: It was the **Club brothers**, the owners of the famouse clinic!

The brothers stood at the edge of the underground lake, pouring horrible-looking **gOO** into the water.

How strange! I sniffed the air, and recognized the smell — it was prehistoric **prune juice**!

Then we heard them laughing. "Ha, ha, ha! Now everyone will have an even worse **stomachache** than we gave them before," said Shifty Club. "They'll think Bluster Conjurat is a **FOOL**, and they'll get

tired of waiting for the chosen one to return from his **MISSION**."

Shady Club laughed. "Hee, hee, hee! He probably won't return anyway. Few ever escape the Cave of Memories alive."

"And then everyone will have to come to the **Club Brothers' Clinic** to be cured!" said Shifty, greedily rubbing his paws together.

What scoundrels!

Trap was so angry that he was ready to jump out of the hiding spot to **confront** them. But I held him back. If we were quiet and followed them, we could find the **EXIT**!

THINK, THINK . . .

My brain sprang into action as we followed the two scoundrels through the **UNDERGROUND** passageway.

Think, think, think . . .

After a little while, I started to get a headache — we cavemice get tired after thinking too much! But everything soon became clear:

1 The Cave of Memories seemed to be **CONNECTED** to Old Mouse City by tunnel.

2 All the WATER in the village came from this underground lake.

3 The Club brothers came from Old Mouse City and poured **prune juice** into the water, so they were responsible for

the **Great Stomachache!**

4 With Trap's help, I had completed my mission and found the recipe for the cure. But we had also discovered the ROTTEN RODENTS behind this epidemic!

5 When I returned to Old Mouse City, I would be greeted as a hero. Surely that would impress *Clarissa Conjurat*, the most **fascinating** rodent in the village!

I was still daydreaming when Trap gave me a **pinch** and brought me back to my senses.

"WAKE UP, COUSIN, this isn't the time for dreaming!" he said.

Trap was right!

Up ahead, the Club brothers were exiting the cave, disappearing into the **night**. We followed, making sure they didn't see us. Just as I had guessed, this tunnel had led us right to *Old Mouse City*.

I took a deep breath of the fresh night air and gazed at the starry sky. How wonderful to be outside and home again!

Trap gave me another pinch. "WAKE UP, COUSIN!"

"Sorry, Trap. I guess the stars are making me feel **romantic** right now," I said.

Whoops! Did I say that out loud?

Trap started to make fun of me. "You're

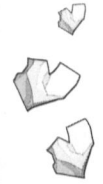

in love! Your heart is softer than cream cheese, Cousin! Who is it? Do I know her?"

I tried to deny it, but my ears turned as **red** as burning lava.

"No, I'm not in love," I protested. "And if I were, I wouldn't tell you who it is! Everyone at the ʀᴏᴛᴛᴇɴ ᴛᴏᴏᴛʜ ᴛᴀᴠᴇʀɴ would know. And that Sally Rockmousen would announce it on her ɢᴏssip ʀᴀᴅio show! Everyone would know that I have an enormouse crush on Clariss —"

I clapped a paw over my mouth, but it was too late.

I'm not sure if Trap figured it out. He didn't say anything, but he gave me a sly look.

I quickly tried to distract him. "That's enough gossip!" I exclaimed. "We have a **MISSION** to complete! The only reason I

didn't get sick today is because my water pipe was broken. So we must **WARN** the city: No one can drink the water that is piped into Old Mouse City until it has been cleaned up."

"How can we warn them all?" Trap asked.

"Go quickly, and wake up all our relatives, all your friends, and all of my employees at *The Stone Gazette*!" I told him. "Tell them to bring their **CHISELS**!"

Trap *ran off*, and soon I had a small army of rodents working with me. We chiseled all night long!

By morning, every well and **WATER** source in the city had a sign on it: **DON'T DRINK! TAINTED WATER!**

Then I took the recipe for the cure to Bluster Conjurat.

"There is a **spring** outside the city that hasn't been tainted," I told him. "You should

107

THE STONE GAZETTE

1. Entrance
2. Reception
3. Rest area
4. Stone tablet storage
5. Editorial office
6. Art Department
7. Geronimo's office

make the chamomile tea with that."

"Thank you, Chosen One!" he said. "You were **brilliant**!"

I looked around the shaman's cave, hoping that Clarissa had heard that compliment. But his **lovely** daughter was nowhere in sight.

So much for romance, I thought, and then yawned. I was exhausted! I went back to my cave for a good night's **sleep**.

HEAD OVER TAIL IN LOVE!

The next morning, I woke up to the sound of Gossip Radio.

"Geronimo Stiltonoot is in love with a mysterious rodent!" Sally Rockmousen was shrieking.

Geronimo is in love?

Who could it be?

Ah, so **Trap** had spilled the beans! *He'll never change*, I thought. But at least he hadn't heard me say *Clarissa's* name.

Then there was a knock on the door, and the entire Heftymouse family **burst** into my cave.

"Who is this mysterious rodent?" Harriet asked. "Is it me?"

This was awkward. "It's just gossip!" I protested. "I'm not in **love** with anybody!"

"Well, I'm not in love with you, either!" Harriet said with a sniff.

Ernest Heftymouse was furious. "**THE WEDDING IS OFF!**" he announced.

My sister's friend's neighbor told me . . .

What a relief! I thought. Then the **pounding** of the village

drums interrupted us.

"Everyone come quickly!" a rodent was shouting. "The shaman has prepared a potion that will cure the **Great Stomachache**!"

I raced to Singing Rock Square, where I saw the Club brothers standing in front of a pot of Bluster's **potion**.

"Cavemice, don't trust Bluster! His **cure** for the Great Stomachache won't work!" squealed Shifty Club. "Come to our clinic. Only we can cure you! And it only costs **one hundred seashells** per rodent!"

I jumped in front of them, furious. "You Stone-Age **scoundrels**! May the Great Zap **strike** your tails!" I yelled.

The whole village was listening. "You two made everyone sick!" I went on. "Yesterday, my cousin Trap and I **saw** you —"

Shady Club interrupted me. "Oh, yes? And how will you prove that we **polluted** the springs?"

I grinned. Shady Club had just confessed without realizing it!

Shifty Club **BOPPED** his brother on the head. "**Quiet, you fool!** You almost revealed all the details of our plan!"

But the angry residents of Old Mouse City had heard enough. They took out their **clubs** and chased the Club brothers out of town. Those brothers didn't show their **WHISKERS** again for a long time!

Then the citizens celebrated my triumph. "**LONG LIVE GERONIMO!**" they cheered. "Long live the chosen one! Long live the hero of Old Mouse City!"

Harriet Heftymouse looked at me and sighed. "I've decided to forgive you, Geronimo. I'll **marry** you after all!"

I took off running.

"Excuse me, I really need to go now," I

shouted behind me. "I have a very **IMPORTANT** appointment!"

I ran to my **OFFICE** and shut myself in. I wanted to preserve this incredible story forever, so I **CHISELED** it into Leo Edistone's new invention — the stone book!

It was the perfect invention for a **storyteller** like me:

Geronimo Stiltonoot, cavemouse!

Don't miss any of my fabumouse adventures!

#1 Lost Treasure of the Emerald Eye

#2 The Curse of the Cheese Pyramid

#3 Cat and Mouse in a Haunted House

#4 I'm Too Fond of My Fur!

#5 Four Mice Deep in the Jungle

#6 Paws Off, Cheddarface!

#7 Red Pizzas for a Blue Count

#8 Attack of the Bandit Cats

#9 A Fabumouse Vacation for Geronimo

#10 All Because of a Cup of Coffee

#11 It's Halloween, You 'Fraidy Mouse!

#12 Merry Christmas, Geronimo!

#13 The Phantom of the Subway

#14 The Temple of the Ruby of Fire

#15 The Mona Mousa Code

#16 A Cheese-Colored Camper

#17 Watch Your Whiskers, Stilton!

#18 Shipwreck on the Pirate Islands

#19 My Name Is Stilton, Geronimo Stilton

#20 Surf's Up, Geronimo!

#21 The Wild, Wild West

#22 The Secret of Cacklefur Castle

A Christmas Tale

#23 Valentine's Day Disaster

#24 Field Trip to Niagara Falls

#25 The Search for Sunken Treasure

#26 The Mummy with No Name

#27 The Christmas Toy Factory

#28 Wedding Crasher

#29 Down and Out Down Under

#30 The Mouse Island Marathon

#31 The Mysterious Cheese Thief

Christmas Catastrophe

#32 Valley of the Giant Skeletons

#33 Geronimo and the Gold Medal Mystery

#34 Geronimo Stilton, Secret Agent

#35 A Very Merry Christmas

#36 Geronimo's Valentine

#37 The Race Across America

#38 A Fabumouse School Adventure

#39 Singing Sensation

#40 The Karate Mouse

#41 Mighty Mount Kilimanjaro

#42 The Peculiar Pumpkin Thief

#43 I'm Not a Supermouse!

#44 The Giant Diamond Robbery

#45 Save the White Whale!

#46 The Haunted Castle

#47 Run for the Hills, Geronimo!

#48 The Mystery in Venice

#49 The Way of the Samurai

#50 This Hotel is Haunted

#51 The Enormouse Pearl Heist

#52 Mouse in Space!

#53 Rumble in the Jungle

Up next!

#54 Get into Gear, Stilton!

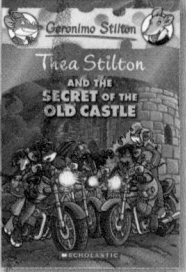

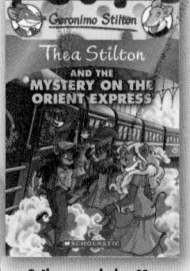

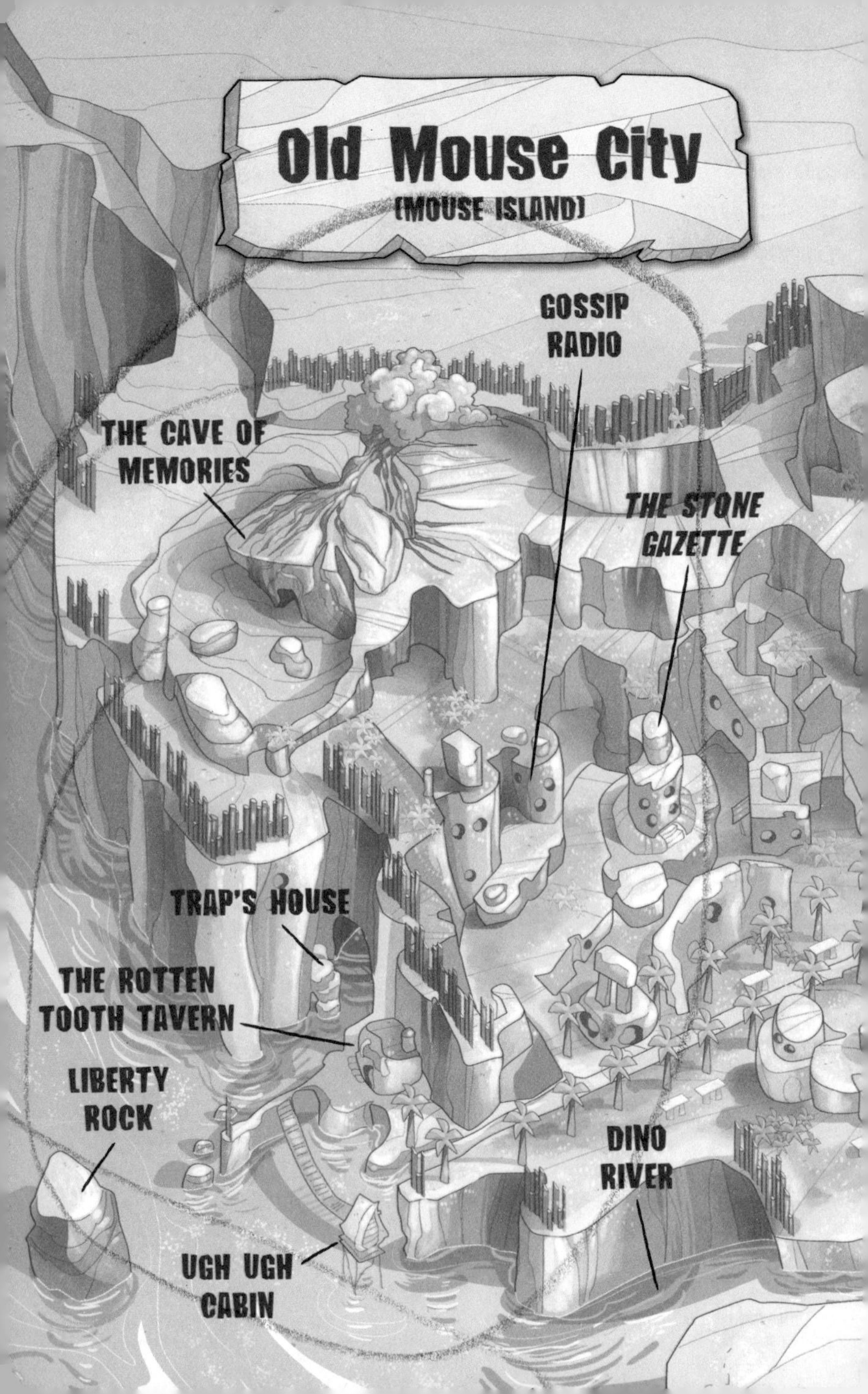

Old Mouse City
(MOUSE ISLAND)

GOSSIP RADIO

THE CAVE OF MEMORIES

THE STONE GAZETTE

TRAP'S HOUSE

THE ROTTEN TOOTH TAVERN

LIBERTY ROCK

DINO RIVER

UGH UGH CABIN

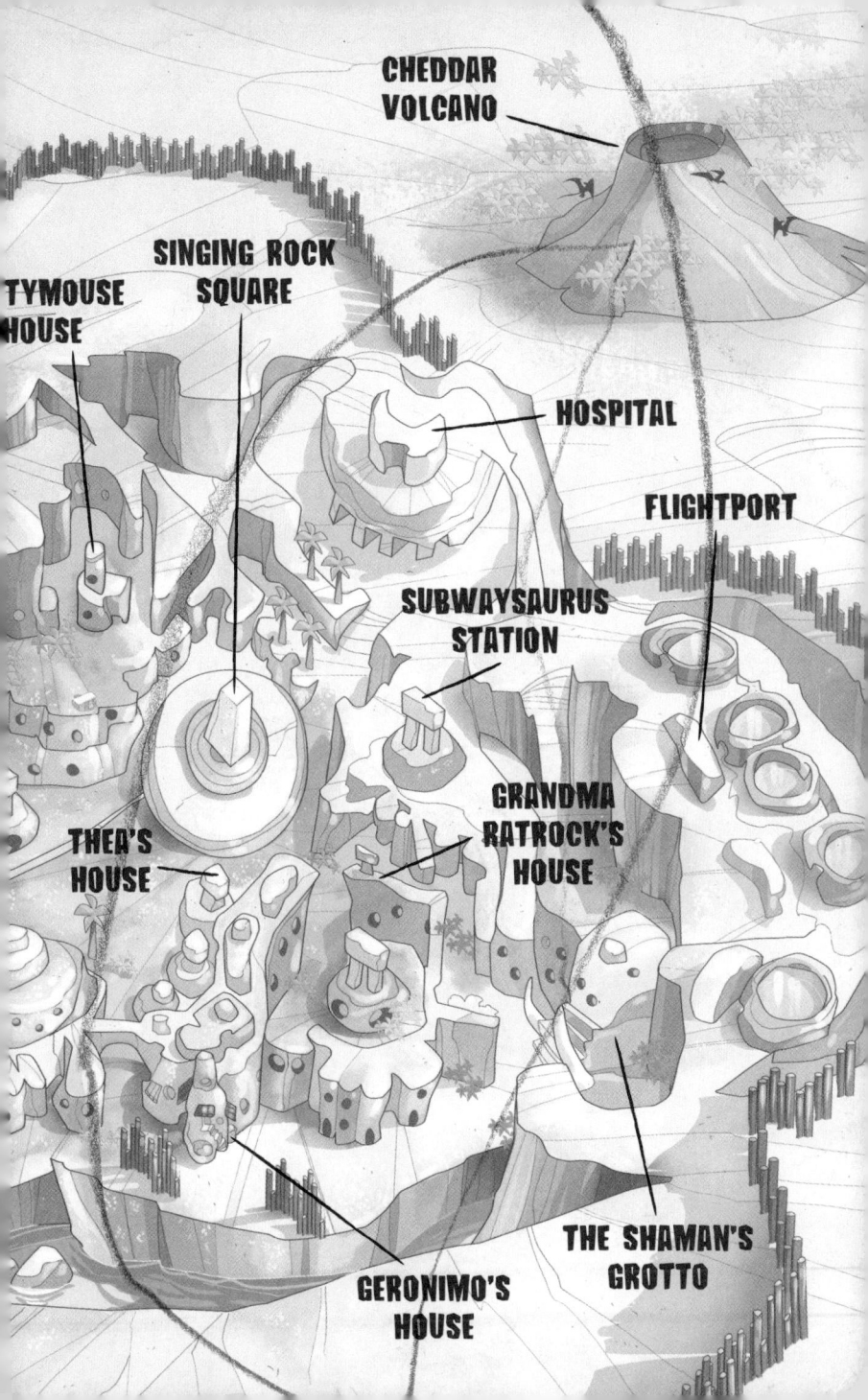